Triple The Surprise

A collection of three rapid pregnancy inspired erotic tales.

Triple The Surprise

Talia Swarky

Published by Talia Swarky, 2021.

TRIPLE THE SURPRISE

First edition. July 20, 2021.

Copyright © 2021 Talia Swarky.

ISBN: 979-8201249168

Written by Talia Swarky.

Also by Talia Swarky

Supernatural Soulmates
Overdue
A Goddess Born
Twins, Tentacles, And Other Squirmy Things
Brandi's Brownie Baby Surprise
One Full Moon
Triple The Surprise
Quick Beats
Popping On The Birthday Stream
The Best Experiment
The Blind Alpha's Pregnant Mate
The Midnight Show

Watch for more at https://books2read.com/ap/nBkZpK/
Talia-Swarky.

Table of Contents

Brandi's Brownie Baby Surprise

"Egg salad Sandwich? Sure. Honey-Cashew Chicken? Yep." I piled all the bowls of stored food on the table next to me, the chill from the office refrigerator's open door raising up a slight chill against my skin. The silky fabric of my new size 4 button up blouse, and my slinky pencil skirt did little against the cold air, but when a girl has a supermodel style figure, you just have to show off.

"Brandi, I don't know how you can eat like that and still be so skinny. There's something seriously wrong with you." My friend and coworker from the cubicle next door, Sharon, shook her head. The classic middle aged housewife with a dumpy figure shrouded in loose blouses and knit pants straining at their hems to contain her thick thighs, Sharon was far from a looker but she made a great lunch partner because she could eat almost as much as I could. "Plus you're literally stealing from your coworkers."

"It's called good genes. That's what blessed me with these." I teased, squishing my generous C cups that strained the fabric of my blouse between my arms while popping off the lid on the chicken. I slid into the chair opposite Sharon and scattered my scavenged lunch across the table. The chicken, a bowl of spaghetti, the sandwich, and a 9 x 13 pan of thick fudgy brownies that had my mouth absolutely watering. "And it's not stealing if no one bothers to put their name on them. It's a community fridge, ya know." I popped one of the crispy fried chicken bites in my mouth, crunching loudly as the sweet and spicy taste flooded my tongue. A little shiver rippled through my shoulders, loosening a few strands of my platinum blonde hair from the bun pinned to the base of my neck.

"What about that one?" Sharon broke off from eating her own disappointing lunch of a wilted green salad sprinkled with ancient looking brown carrot slivers and scrawny red peppers to point a fork at the pan of brownies. "That one specifically says 'Brandi, do not eat!' in big, bold letters taped to a note on top?"

I reached over, flicking the yellow sticky note with my name with the tip of my finger and watched the paper flutter its way to the floor. "What note?" I smiled, my white teeth flashing against the crimson red of my lip-gloss, and popped another chunk of chicken into my mouth. My empty stomach let out a long squeaking rumble, protesting its current empty state, and I smoothed my palm down over my flat belly, stretching the silk until I could see the indentation of my navel and the bump of my belly button ring. "Don't worry, I'm going to fill you up so full that you won't have room to even make a squeak."

By the time the lunch bell rang, every scrap of my lunch was currently packed into my belly. Creating a slight rounded bulge that pleasantly tightened my shirt across my swollen and stuffed belly, it gurgled thickly beneath my hands, a small burp leaking up my throat and out of my lips. I teetered back to my cubicle, my six inch heels clicking loudly against the tile floor, and ignored the stares of my coworkers when I sank down into the cushy confines of my chair with a long and very loud moan. A dull ache had started deep in my ribs, my heart faintly throbbing in my ears as my belly sloshed and groaned with each breath, a shivering wave spreading underneath my skin as the overfilled organ struggled to process my meal. "What's wrong, belly? You've eaten so much more before." I kneaded my knuckles against a tender spot along the right side of my ribs, a loud sound like bubbles popping splashed around and a grumble roared under my hand. Another burp forced its way out of my throat, leaving the taste of soured chocolate and something else metallic clinging to my tongue. Yuck!

"I told you shouldn't eat those things!" Sharon's mousy head popped over my cubicle wall, scowling like she was my mother or something. "You've probably got food poisoning or something."

"Shut up! I don't get food poisoning, I can eat anything I want!" I snarled, hunching over my desk with one arm folded over my churning belly, staring determinedly at the piles of papers waiting for my signature and approval. I could do this. I could. There was nothing wrong with my belly. Nothing at all.

I hope.

2

"Oh, god. Belly, what is wrong with you?" I groaned, tightly clutching my hands across the rounded, groaning mass of my belly. The ache that had started deep in my ribs spread all across the surface, sharp pains running down from the top of my stomach all the way down to my crotch. It was bulging, small square diamonds of pale flesh peeking through the buttons of my shirt straining to contain it. It felt so heavy, pressing out against my hands with a thick warm pressure right behind my navel, and my soft skin was turning harder. So hard that my fingers could barely make a dent in it. I wish I could burp, the intense pressure felt like it would let up then. But no matter how hard I kneaded my hands into the tender spots, nothing would come out.

A second moan lingered long and low out of my throat, and I faintly heard a few rushed whispers along with a moan of satisfaction from behind my cubical wall. The wet sound of skin slapping on skin was unmistakable, and the self-satisfied male moan was echoed by a thick churning gurgle that rolled through my belly. Oh, god. Creepy John from behind me was getting off to my moans.

"Oh! Please, belly. You've got to stop!" I groaned, my eyes flashing down to the clock at the corner of my computer screen. Two more minutes. Two more minutes until I could leave here and be in the privacy of my own car. A thick cramp squeezed down like a vise on my poor abused belly, and I nearly screamed in pain as my head twisted back and forth against the edge of my chair. My hair was pulled free, tangling around my head in a thick blonde wad and caked with sweat. Thick circles of dampness had formed under my arms and even spread across my breasts, the silky fabric of my shirt sticking to every curve of my heavy breasts and brightly illuminating the hardened nubs of my nipples poking up through the fabric of my lacy bra. They scratch against the fabric, sending little electric waves of pleasure straight down to my pussy that was damping as well.

With every breath that bounced my heavy chest up and down, a thick sloshing gurgle churned in the rounded pudge of my belly. I leaned back into the full grip of my chair, letting it bulge forward as the waistband painfully tight waist band dug into my skin, catching on the tip of my belly ring. Another moan crept out of my throat as I rubbed my hands over my belly, the pressure easing a little but it wasn't enough. The painful tightness was still there, and something else too. Gentle nudges from deep inside me, they push out against my hands and draw more whines out of my throat.

I look at the screen again, and right there by the little clock that said 5:00 p.m. is a new message. Sender unknown.

Brandi,

You're always so beautiful with your trim figure and beautiful smile, but all that beauty hides a nasty personality that doesn't give a single fuck for anyone. Always humiliating people and stealing their food. Maybe now since you're growing a person inside you, you'll finally get a clue on how to treat others with respect. Hope you enjoy your rapid pregnancy as much as you enjoyed those brownies. We'll certainly enjoy watching you.

Signed, your friendly coworkers.

My mouth dropped open in horror, a silent scream of horror rounded my lips. No! There was no way I could be pregnant!

Losing my cute, flat little belly and growing some kind of disgusting baby deep inside me. There was no way in hell I was having this!

"You all did this! You all wanted to ruin me!" I screamed out to the ceiling, my eyes rolling around to see so many familiar faces peeking over my cubicle wall, each one watching the growing bump of my lower belly as it swells out with each breath. My elbows shove back against the chair arms, a gurgle of protest echoing from my stomach, and I try to sit up but the weight pushes me back down.

Then I hear it.

The strain of fabric ripping apart stitch by stitch until it finally gives out.

POP

3

The buttons on my blouse popped off one by one, hitting the ceiling with a loud ping, and bounced off the tiles. The button on my skirt followed right behind, hitting one of my lurking coworkers right in the eye. My belly surges forward, a swollen mound of pale flesh spilling out into my lap. Another moan spills out of my mouth, the heavy warmth stretching my poor belly out like a woman six months pregnant. It's too much. I can't take it.

"Please make it stop! Please make my poor belly stop!" Tears welled up in my eyes as a thick burn started to strain my skin, jagged red stripes appearing up and down the thick ball of my belly. Stretch marks, I belatedly thought. My belly is ruined. The soft little nudges that felt like bubbles popping inside me hardened as the baby grew, shivers rippling across the skin as it jolted deep inside me, pressing out harder time and time again with each one growing stronger. A particularly strong jolt shoved my belly up against my breasts, shaking loose a thickened drop of something from my tender nipples. I heard a gasp rippling through the groan, and I craned my neck to see not just one drop, but twin splotches spreading across the lacy fabric of my bra.

"Leaking slightly, are we Brandi?"

Mr. Brandsfield, my boss, stepped right in front of me. All long legs and lean muscle, the raw swimmer's muscles were highlighted by the tight fitting silk of his dress shirt. Like a panther on the hunt, he prowled forward and reached out one large hand, smoothing over the tight skin and an instant curl of heat rippled down through my core. I could feel myself start to drip, my heart pounding harder against my chest, and he flashes a predatory smile of perfect white teeth.

"Enjoying yourself, are we? I thought you would." A breathy moan flutters out of my throat as his hands rise up, kneading into my swelling milk filled breasts. My eyes fall shut as my spine arches, pushing my chest more into his delicious torture, and my core clenches needfully against the empty air. A second lingering pass of his fingers brushes over my belly that grows bigger with each passing moment, pushing the remains of my blouse open wider until there's nothing but a belly rounding out like I swallowed a ball.

My hips grind down against my chair, desperate for something to relieve the empty ache between my thighs, but there's nothing but empty air. His hand slid up my thigh, the tips of his fingers lightly grazed over my pussy, and my eyes barely fluttered open to see every eye in the office trained on me. Or more specifically on Mr. Brandsfield's hand tugging down my lacy thong. The cold air bit against the wetness coating my lips, a hiss sliding between my teeth, but it was quickly replaced by the rough warmth of his fingers curling up into my core.

"Not much longer now," His hand smoothed over my navel as it popped out, no room left for it to stay inside now. The baby's too large, filling up everything south from my breasts to my hips. The head shifts, settling deep in my hips, and I can feel it start to drop. A sharp pain squeezed my womb, so intense that a few tears squeezed out of my eyes, and a single finger dragged so slowly over my clit that my back arched despite the pain. My lips rounded out in a howl, my womb clenching around the invading push of his fingers, circling around, pulling back. My hips started to grind down into the chair, the wet slap of his fingers sliding through my soaking lips only increasing the tight knot of pressure deep in my core. "Your pregnancy is coming to a head it seems, literally." He chuckled softly, but I couldn't care less at the moment. I had to find something to release that pressure. "Now hop up on your table."

"Huh?" I blinked, my mind too hazy to think just right.

"I said we were going to enjoy you and your pregnancy, Brandi. Every single moment." His fingers slid out of my pussy with a wet squelch, pointing to my desk which was rapidly being cleared by a guy whose pants were nearly ripping at the crotch from being so hard.

"No! No, I can't!" I protested, but it died in a long drawn out moan, clutching my belly as the hardest pain yet squeezed my belly. Was this contractions? Was the baby already coming out?

"Yes, you will!" Grabbing my arms away from my belly, he pulled me up on my shaky legs. The entire room tilts, filled with too many faces all eagerly looking at me. My eyes roam around the room, seeing far too many hands rubbing crotches and fingers disappearing under skirts, and the tears start to fall harder. They're actually enjoying this, seeing me so miserable and ruined. This gigantic belly hanging out in front of me and twitching with the contractions. It's too much. Mr. Brandsfield's hand skimmed down, dragging over my clit as he pushed me forward to my desk. "Now get up there and show us that pretty pregnant pussy!"

My stomach curled up as another contraction hit, the head grating against my hip bones as I wobbled to the desk. Each step was a swinging dance that nearly let me fall forward on my face, but I made it. My fingers latched on tight to the edge, the entire flimsy table shaking as my swollen belly brushed against the side. The baby wriggled as the bump of my navel scraped against the surface, arching pinpricks of electricity pooling down into my spine as I balanced on all fours. It's coming, the baby's coming. I can feel it sliding down. My throat hurts when I moan so hard that it ends in a scream, the pressure so intense that it felt like my hips were about to break, and then something does. A rush of fluid surges down my legs, slapping down onto the desk and pooling around my knees. It's clear and odorless, not like the thick milk soaking into my bra.

It's my water. My water just broke.

4

"**E**veryone, get ready for the show!" I felt his hands spread my thighs wide, too wide for me to even try and hide anything as the pain suddenly got so much worse. Wave after wave, another one crashing down on my core before the other fully left was pulling me open inside. My womb opening up and shoving this baby out of me, this wiggling thing pulling itself out of me. I gritted my teeth, the urge to push curling my hands into the surface of the desk for support.

"It's coming out!" A broken cry ripped out of my throat, my pussy bulging out into a teardrop shape that I could feel stretched too thin, then slowly, slowly parting open to let the head drop out. Pure fire singed every nerve down there, a murmur of applause rippled behind my back, and the painful push of the contractions forced the blocky shoulders out next. My slender thighs trembled with exhaustion, so sticky with sweat and fluid that it felt like I'd never be clean again.

Weaker than before, but still strong enough that I screamed, the finishing wave of contractions clamped down on my womb and forced the rest of the baby out. Landing with a sickening wet smack into a pair of waiting hands, a round of smattered applause broke out as my arms gave out and I fell down onto my stomach, my legs sliding off the desk and banging sharply against the floor.

"Well, Ladies and Gentlemen. I believe that we have witnessed a beautiful rapid pregnancy from Ms. Brandi. Wouldn't you say?" A murmur of approval rippled through the crowd and I felt my heart sink. I was ruined, my perfect self ruined. Looking down, I saw my breasts had swollen, bulging over the edge of my soaked bra and leaking milk in thick creamy white streams down my chest. My beautiful little flat belly that could eat anything was gone, swollen out like I was still six months pregnant and streaked with these horrible red marks. The tip of my navel ring engorged deep into my skin that was still twitching slightly with the aftershocks of so much abuse. Fluid of some sort still squished out of my pussy, racing down my legs stained with drying birth fluids. It was horrible, I've never been so embarrassed before.

And that's what they wanted. They wanted me to be this way. My eyes rolled up, taking note of each one of the smiling faces pointing and laughing at me like I was some carnival freak show. And then there was Mr. Brandsfield. Tall, sexy Mr. Brandsfield that was holding that crying baby high like it was some sort of trophy. It's kinda funny how much it looked like him.

Maybe since they all enjoyed my humiliating pregnancy so much, they might just get one of their own. I'd make sure of that.

Tea For Two

I probably shouldn't have chugged the whole pitcher.

My stomach gurgled wetly, the bloated curve of my belly bulging out from the pitcher of special Fertili-tea I had bought off the internet for just the low, low, price of $9.99. Real results in less than 15 minutes, it promised. A small laugh bubbled up in my throat, and I curled my hand through the damp strands of my dark curly hair. It was kind of funny if you think about it. How my fiancée, Milo, was always talking about how he wanted a big family, and now I was going to give it to him just as quickly as I could.

Before I had gulped down the special tea that would make my barely there pregnancy a whole lot more obvious, I had made sure we had sex several times right at my magic time. The online bidding store that sold the tea made sure to say that it would only work if you were pregnant beforehand, and I made triple sure that everything had taken root before I took the tea. The six pink sticks still littering the countertop confirmed that very clearly for me. Now I was laying in my tub, completely bare except for the water with my soft pink nipples quickly puckering firm from the cool air, and my thick thighs parted to let the reflection of my lower lips showing in the mirror across from my tub.

If the bubbling, sloshing sounds from my stomach were any indication, the tea was working its magic.

A slight smile curved up the edges of my lips as my eyes never left the soft pudginess of my belly, slowly starting to swell up with each breath I took. Being a curvy girl of a size 16, I was pretty used to all the bulges that came with being a larger size, but there was something almost thrilling about watching my belly rise up in front of my eyes. The quick pop-pop of what felt like bubbles inside moving around made me want to laugh, and I eagerly reached down to glide my fingers over the small pale swell. The flutter was growing stronger, shifting around low in my belly, and I let out a small moan as a curl of heat warmed my core and sent a small nervous shiver coiling through my insides.

Maybe I should have thought this through a little more.

Scooting back to get a little more comfortable, the growing weight in my belly had started to make itself known. Pressing down on my spine like I had overeaten at a buffet, just minus the belly ache. If anything, my belly felt a little warmer than normal. Not bad or anything, but a pleasant warmth. It must be the special pregnancy stuff in the tea that made it so pleasant feeling. I swirled my fingertip over my navel, traveling up towards my breasts and pressing in softly to feel for my Fundal Height. It was kind of funny to feel the firm little knob of my Uterus just stop and turn back into soft jiggly skin.

Then I heard it, my phone started to ring.

"Hey, Manda baby! The shop's kinda slow tonight, so I was wondering what you were doing?" The cheerful voice on the other end sounded like a ray of sunshine, sweet as honey and bubbly as a hot spring. I could just see him now, one lazy leg crossed over the other, his toe jiggling impatiently while he scribbled a random doodle on anything he had laying loose. His kissably plump lower lip would be slightly flushed from his teeth worrying it, and the lime green and golden yellow dragon tattoo curling up his neck would be partially hidden by a few overlong strands of his long ebony hair. His hazel eyes would be dancing, the golden flecks shimmering with the blossoming idea of some artwork in his brilliant mind.

"Hey yourself," A long moan spilled out of my lips as I leaned back down into the water, a warm surge pulling my belly out into a bulge worthy of five months pregnant. It was really starting to round out now, not just a fat pot belly but a real rounded belly like I was pregnant. "I was just taking a bath."

"Yeah, I can tell. Sounds like you were having a little fun while you were in there. That's pretty cruel considering that I'm stuck here and missing out." Milo's voice pitched a little lower, like he was muffling something with his hand. "Unless you're up for a little frisky fun?"

"You know me, always ready for your magic touch." God that sounded cheesy. But I couldn't help it. This simmering heat down in my core was getting stronger. I pushed the speakerphone and put the phone back on the counter, the soft hiss of his breathing echoing through the speaker, it made me want to hear the way it stuttered when he came. My fingers ghosted over my breasts, my nipples firm against a tentative swirl of touch. Mmm... So good.

"Damn, baby!" His laugh floats through the air like a cloud, my thighs flexing together to try and relieve a little bit of the ache. "I wish that was my hands gliding over your beautiful body. Tell me, where would you like it? My hands gliding over your sides? Or maybe you'd like my lips, just barely touching yours while my fingers curl over those thick thighs I love so much. Slowly lowering, teasing over that sweet pussy of yours. All nice and wet, just for me. Shit, just thinking of you laying there, all flushed and pretty. It's got my heart pounding and my cock's hard. I wish you could feel me babe."

"I *know*," I swallowed thickly, a roll of hunger so strong that it felt like it would rip me apart rocked through my core. Another swirl of my fingertips around my nipples, and I swear I could feel my breasts growing heavier, fuller with something. My breath hitched hard, a high pitched whine seeping through the firmly pressed line of my lips, and I swear I heard Milo groan that special way. Fueled by the tea, my belly was really rounding out now. Sticking out from my body like a partially inflated basketball, it gave me an idea on just how he could see what I was doing for him. "Milo," Reaching out for my phone, I flipped the camera on and flicked the live chat on. The little red light in the corner of the screen flipped on, and the swollen curve of my belly suddenly filled the screen. "I want your hands here. On my belly that's growing a baby just for you."

A clatter came through the phone, rattles and chinks finally ending in a single thud. It sounded like he dropped the phone, and I arched one eyebrow in concern.

"Milo? You okay?"

"You're pregnant? You're fucking pregnant?"

"How? You weren't pregnant this morning... were you?" Milo's voice dipped low at the end, curiosity drawing out every syllable until I was cackling.

"Mm-hm. I was already pregnant thanks to all that cum you've pumped in me the last few weeks, but this special tea I bought off the internet is helping speed things along." Something low in my belly shifted, a ripple of movement causing the twitching mass of my belly to start to bounce up and down like a bowl of gelatin. The baby was moving. "Look what you've done to me. Got me all swollen up. My belly, my breasts. I'll probably start leaking any moment. And I'm so wet. Can you see, baby?" Lowering the camera down, I spread my lips with two fingers. Letting him see just how swollen my clit, swollen and throbbing for a touch.

"Yeah, I can see." His voice was breathless, gasping. The clink of his belt loosening and the hiss of a zipper snaked over the connection. I could almost see him in my mind, his ink stained fingers folded around his cock, fisting himself up and down at that perfect pace he liked so much. Not too fast or too slow. My fingers crept a little higher, the wet squelch and the burning stretch of my fingers sinking in up to my knuckles drawing out a sigh. Milo's answering moan and a whispered rush of my name came a heartbeat later, sending my hips rocking against the heavy weight of the baby pinning them down.

"I'm so big now," Raising my eyes to my belly, the massive mound bulged out from my belly like a giant pumpkin and twitching softly with every one of the baby's slow movements.

With no room left inside, my navel had bulged out in a pink nub not unlike my nipples and just as sensitive. I pulled the camera back up nearly to my chin, letting him see just how a few creamy white droplets of milk were starting to spill out from my nipples, and how the muscles in my belly were twitching with every circle of my fingertip against my fat clit. "This. This is what you did to me, Milo. Feel proud?"

Something thudded against a hard surface. His head slamming against something? He was panting, the slick sounds of his hand sliding up and down his cock so loud that I could hear it plainly through my speaker. Faster, harder. Needing to come. Just like I was. My spine arched, the coil of heat tightening low in my core, and then I came. A clenching wave of heat and energy that had every muscle shaking and my head swimming. Instead of the pure bliss that I was expecting, a sharp pain lanced right through my belly. Musky scented fluid gushed over my fingers, clear but sticky, and I let out a groan as my eyes shut tight. This wasn't right. I've never had an orgasm that felt like my belly was about to explode.

"Milo?" My voice trembled, pitching higher with fear as the cramp clamped down on my belly like a white hot band.

His breath stuttered, taking a moment to come down from his high, before I heard him swallow heavily. "What's wrong, Amanda?" He was struggling to breathe normally, but each one seemed to bring him more alert.

The baby let out a hard kick, the weight of my belly shifting so low in my hips. "I think I'm in labor!"

"**S**hit! Just keep still... Um." Something metallic clattered, like keys hitting his desk. "I'm locking up the shop. J-Just stay there, and I'll be right home!"

"It's coming! I can't." Another cramp slammed down onto my core before the last one ended. The baby's head was jamming low in my hips, grating harshly down my canal as inch by inch it came closer to bulging out of my lips. I whimpered, lowering the phone down with my shaky hands so he could see my swollen lips. "Here, watch."

The mixture of sweat, my cum, and the water left my thighs glistening as I pushed them as far apart as I could. It was coming too fast. I cupped my free hand down, feeling the hot warmth of my lips starting to stretch. To bulge out into a teardrop shape as each contraction forced me open. Milo jabbered something, the audio crackling with the mishmash of sounds, and something soft and slick brushed against my fingers. The head, my mind screamed at me, my baby's head.

I pushed down again, screaming until my throat was raw as my raw core burned like fire was flaring in my hips. A sickening pop that made my stomach flop uneasily, and then the weight of something slid free. Soft, slick skin brushed against the sensitive inner side of my thighs, and I guided the weight out and gently lifted it to my chest. The baby, my baby, fluid streaked but whole instantly nestled against my chest. All tiny wriggly limbs and squinted eyes. My heart swelled up double and I made sure to get the camera tilted for the best angle so that Milo could see.

"Hurry home soon, baby. Someone wants to meet you."

Pepperoni Pizza And A Date Night Triplet Surprise

1

Asoft knock at the door told me that my dinner had finally arrived. The extra-large pepperoni, sausage, ham, and cheddar pizza was just what I had been craving for the last few days. My stomach rumbled, growling out so loud that I nearly jumped out of my skin. My heart kicked up a pounding tempo in my chest, and I flattened one hand against the gently swollen curve of my bare belly. I had been out shopping all day, and I was so thirsty that I came home and guzzled an entire pitcher of lemonade before changing into my favorite lace lingerie. My boyfriend, Sebastian, was due back any minute, and I wanted to surprise him with take out tonight.

It was a good thing I ordered in because I certainly wasn't fit to go out. My normally flat stomach was all pushed out from the lemonade, a neat little rounded ball that stretched the artful black lace draping down from my full C cup breasts. Beneath the lace of my long gown, it sloshed and jiggled each time I took a step. Little miniature waves crested and crashing around inside me, gurgling heavily beneath my hand as I gave it a little pat and went to the door.

"Um... Hello? I-I have your order." The delivery boy standing there with a huge cardboard box in hand blanched so white that I could see every ginger freckle on his cheeks. His eyes nearly bulged out of their sockets, exposing white rims as they traced down every inch of my exposed curves. Barely flickering over my face and the waterfall of straight raven hair that I had let fall freely about my shoulders, he seemed enchanted by the way my slender golden shoulders poked out of the long scarlet lace gown. The tie rested just around my neck, halter style, and the lace was certainly see through as it draped from my chest to my ankles. A few artful swirls just barely covered the tips of my nipples that were quickly stiffening from the cool bite of the air, and a different set swirled down around my lower lips. Whatever else he was required to say died on his tongue as he jabbered a garbled mish-mash of words, and I couldn't help but toss my head back and laugh while shoving the money in his hands.

"Thanks a lot! Have a good evening." I chirped ever so cheerfully, snatching the pizza box out of his hand and kicking the door closed with my foot. Poor guy, he'd probably have blue balls for a while now.

Just as I put the pizza box on the table, I heard a beep coming from my phone on the couch. My lips pushed up in a slight pout. That was odd. I wasn't expecting anything. Curious, I walked over and swiped my finger across the screen, Sebastian's name popping up right away along with his newest message. He was stuck in traffic and was going to be late for our date. A sharp pang of disappointment stabbed my chest at the same time my stomach let out a noisy growl, the lemonade hadn't done much to soothe my hunger, and now I had this delicious smelling pizza right here. He surely would mind if I took a tiny bite.

My fingers flashed as I typed out a quick reply, and the lace swirled around my legs as I dashed to the table and lifted the pizza, box and all, and wandered over to the couch. It was so large that the box hung off on both sides of my thighs, a few puddles of darker grease starting to soak through the flimsy white cardboard. As soon as I flipped up the lid, the delicious cheesy, meaty smell floated straight up my nose. My eyes fluttered closed in pure delight, my mouth watering from pure excitement, and my wobbly belly squeezed in on the lemonade before letting out a lingering squeak.

2

Oh. My. God.

I groaned, my arms curling around the swollen, hot bulge of my belly. Impossibly full and tight to the point that it felt like my ribs were about to burst, my stomach aches so badly that it was one solid ball of dull pain, gurgling so loudly that I could feel it churning beneath my hands. Sweat trickled down my neck, slicking my hair down into a matted mess right against skin, and a few stuck to my cheeks. I was so hot, so hot that I had taken off my gown and sat there completely bare. What was wrong with me?

"Oh... You've got to stop!" Leaning back against the sofa, my hands rubbed long strokes from the deep indentation of my navel all the way back up. There weren't any burps in there, not even a single tender spot that I could need my fingers into, but it just hurt so *bad*. A red flush had spread across my skin, and the entire heavy weight felt like an elephant was pushing back up on my lungs. I swear I could feel my heart beating right through my belly, it was slamming against my chest so why not, and I groaned again. Trying to curl my knees up against my chest, but the thick mass in my belly wouldn't let me. Then it started pulsing, the muscles tensing from the strain to hold all this food, and I thought for sure I was going to burst.

Then it moved.

Like a bubble moving under my skin, I let out a shriek as it started shifting around underneath my hand. A red hot cramp sliced through the muscles, shaking the breath out of my chest, and I can feel something bulging. Rising like hot dough, my belly starts growing beneath my hands. Growing, stretching, the muscles burning with a deep ache I could feel in my bones. My hands splayed over my rounding belly, low sloshing gurgles crashing against each other inside my overfilled stomach with each one of my short breaths. I let out a low keening groan, letting my head flop limply back and toss side to side. It hurt so bad. Why wouldn't this stop?

"Baby, what's the matter? You sound like you're in pain."

Opening my eyes just in time to see Sebastian's tall figure glide into the room with his briefcase and cane still in hand, his elegantly carved face was crinkled up in a heavy scowl. His broad shoulders and slender waist were only emphasized by the slightly uneven hang of his suit jacket, and the wrinkled fabric of his white dress shirt had come unbuttoned at the collar. Showing off a hint of sculpted collarbones and hinting at the golden skin that laid beneath, he looked slightly harried. Frustrated maybe, and he let out a soft sigh and ran his free left hand through the chocolate waves of his hair. Even now, with my belly feeling like it was about to explode, a restless curl of heat shifted through my core, and I let out another whimper. "It's cause I am. My belly's hurting so badly! I'm think I'm going to pop!"

"Sounds like you ate too much again." He chuckled wryly to himself, a sparkle of amusement sliding through the deep sea colored pools of his blind eyes. Turning away, I was granted a tantalizing view of his firmly muscled rear as he placed both items on a small table at the entrance. Oh, god. My hips started to grind down against the sofa as the heat grew hotter, sweat trickling down between my breasts that were slowly growing larger too.

"Something's wrong with me! My belly's growing! Come here and see." It must have been the alarm in my voice that made him believe that something was really wrong, but Sebastian turned around with his scowl deeper than ever. Easily shedding his jacket with a shivering roll of his shoulders, he padded towards me with an easy grace.

"You on the couch?"

"Yes!" My spine arched as another lightning pain shot straight through my belly, the movement inside pushing out harder. Kicking almost, and my belly bulged out to the size of a woman six months pregnant. So big that my navel was pulling flat, the pressure wasn't letting up anywhere. Not down at my lips, or in my belly, and certainly not in my chest. My cute little nipples were already turning darker, my breasts swelling at least another cup in size. Whatever was growing inside me was definitely alive, pushing against my ribs and battering my grumbling stomach with heavy blows. My stomach lurched under my hands, desperately trying to push everything back up my throat.

"You okay, honey?" The sofa dipped as he sat down beside me, reaching out with one hand until his fingertips brushed against the tight skin of my belly. "Whoa! You're huge!" The tight bulge didn't even dent when he traced his fingers in a long slow sweep from each side of my ribcage to the other, a tight squeak coming out from deep within my overstuffed stomach, and the movement shifted closer to his hand. I swear I could feel his confused gaze flashing down my face, sensually sliding over my heavy breasts, and stopping at the highest curve of my belly. My thighs rubbed against one another when the tip of his tongue darted out to trace his full lower lip, a slight wetness starting to seep against the tender skin of my thighs. God, how could one man be so sexy? "Did your belly just... move?"

"I think so." The whimper died in my throat as my expanding belly pushed out into his hand. My heart was pounding in anticipation, eager for the way his touch drifted lower and lower, closer to the base of my belly and the dark curls slowly growing slick. My breathing started to grow sharper, faster. The heavy weight of my belly shifting back up into my chest as it grew, and the weight of my breasts pressed down, aching with the need to release something. "It hurts so bad."

"Where? Where does it hurt?" Sebastian's voice deepened to a husky whisper, those magic eyes sliding up and down my body again in that sexy shivering way to catch whatever hints of my body he could see, and my spine involuntary arched forward. Pushing out my breasts and thrusting out my belly, a small whisper of his name fell from my lips just from the pure warmth of his touch. His pupils dilated, staining the intense blue with a spread of ink so dark that my breath hitched in my chest, and the movement inside rolled straight into his touch. Kicking out so hard that my stretched navel popped completely out in one fat pink nub, my belly sloshed and wobbled like a bowl of jelly. "Damn! You're pregnant. You're really pregnant!" He murmured softly in awe, and I knew it. Deep down in my heart, I knew that somehow I really was pregnant.

3

"But how? Even though we did have sex last night, a rapid pregnancy wouldn't take hold unless..." He wandered off, his brows knitting down in deep thought while his hands glided over the tight underswell of my belly. It was so firm now, my skin not giving an inch except where it was growing and the baby moved. "Unless you were already pregnant." He finally finished in a soft whisper.

Nearly the size of a woman at a full nine months, the massive mound weighed down on my legs as it not only swelled from the side, but from the front too. Taking on a torpedo shape, I could feel my skin stretching impossibly more with every breath. A fine spiderweb of dark veins started to stretch across my skin, a subtle glow starting to shimmer across the expanse of my belly, and my pushed out navel turned dark. A Linea Nigra appeared just under the swell of my breasts and ran all the way down to the top of my lips. My nipples turned even darker as well, the pressure mounting inside was too much, and a few drops of creamy white milk leaked from the tips to splatter down on my belly.

"Oh, shit. I'm leaking!"

The wandering hands leave my belly to curl up and cup my breasts, the pad of his thumb brushing over my nipples just right. My heart starts to pound in my chest, slamming against my bones as he makes one torturous circle and then another. The milk slips out, moistening the skin of his hands until they let out a soft smacking sound with each tug and twist. Fanning the embers heating my blood, I can feel the hardness of his cock growing firm against my thigh, and one glance up confirms it.

A sultry hunger lingers over his face, and it takes everything in me not to reach up and smash my lips against his. Instead, I rip my fingers up from where they had curled in the sofa and weave them through his hair. The delighted sounds that came from his throat sent the fire brewing in my core into a full blaze, and my thighs started to rub together just to feed a little more friction against my dripping lips.

"Damn, you're so hot." My leaking nipples tighten against his fingers every time he drifts over them, breaking only a moment to sling off his shirt and send it flying into some forgotten corner to find later. His pants follow a heartbeat later, leaving him in nothing but his tight navy boxers that do nothing to hide the hard length of him at all. My gaze drifts up to trace what my hands can't reach. Over the broad chest lightly tanned and smooth that heaves with every one of his heavy breaths, across the defined curve of his pecs and down the small trail of curled hair that leads below the waistband of his boxers. My tongue trails over my lower lip, a curl of hunger swirling through my overstuffed belly aches for more, but it's not food it wants. It's him. "Never thought I would love you like this." His words are rough and sharp, like he can barely grate them out, but I don't care.

Sebastian leans back down, one hand wrapping around the nape of my neck while the other slides over my still growing belly, dipping down to find out just how wet I am. "Need you. Need you now!" I barely manage to whimper out when his long finger curls inside me. My hands fly up to his waist, digging into the firm muscles of his abs that shift and twitch under my touch. His hips push down, letting me feel the full weight of his hard cock against my entrance. Mine rock back just as eagerly, desperately grinding for the friction I was aching for so badly. The shifting presence of the baby slowly shifts into three distinctive mounds of pressure that kick and squirm out against his torso.

"Just let me grab a taste first." My back arches as his head dips, my lips rounding up into a soundless o as he latches on to my full breasts. The pressure of his lips and tongue nearly sends me screaming, and the added swirl of his fingers over my clit makes my pounding heart speed up even more. My breath snaps out of my lungs, a different sort of pressure contacting the muscles in my bulging belly, but it's too much. The tickle of his hair against my heated skin, the pull of his lips and tongue, the ropes of pleasure tightening in my core. White stars burst behind my eyes, a soothing wave of sweet relief searing down my veins, and a formless jabber of his name fell from my lips. I can feel him growl, rumbling straight through my chest. Blearily I blink down, reaching up to cup his cheek where his milk stained lips curl up in a delighted smile.

"C'mere. Kiss me." He gladly obliges, eagerly pressing his lips to mine while his hand neatly guides his cock right through my folds. The stretch burns, but it's a good one. The type that lets me feel every one of his veins and curves. His first thrust has me keening into his mouth, the second curls my arms as tightly as I can around his shoulders. One hand drops down to my ribs, kneading into the swollen mass of my belly right where one of the babies is kicking out. As if I hadn't come just a few heartbeats ago, the ache in my core starts to grow again. Pulsing out like a wave, I can feel the strange shivers and the tightening in my belly constrict with every one of his thrusts. Pumping almost as fast as my heart, I let my head fall back as he leaves a trail of sticky openmouthed kisses down my neck and chest.

My eyes shut.

The tension breaks.

My insides shiver and shake, the orgasm ripping through my core like a storm. My heavy breasts clench, streams of milk smearing across Sebastian's chest as he keeps thrusting, pushing himself inside me so far that it feels like he's touching my brain. His features blur, my eyes falling shut, but then I feel it. The twitch of his cock inside me, and then he comes. Massively. The thick slap of his balls against my ass turns wetter, sticker as his cum drips out of my overfilled lips. His hips stutter, almost like his breathing, and then his strong arms shake. I don't have the strength to catch him, but he manages to land aside as he crashes down on the sofa.

"Beautiful, baby. Just beautiful." He coos, planting another kiss right above my racing heart, but I barely feel the love in his touch. Instead, my swollen belly bulges forward, and drops down. Each baby feels like the size of a large watermelon, my belly so huge that I can't see anything but shiny stretched skin past my heavy breasts, and then they move. I let out a little squeak of surprise as the weight shifts so low that I can feel something scraping against my hip bones. The overtaxed muscles stiffening with a contraction so strong that I can feel something break inside me.

"Oh my God!" The scream rips out of my throat as a surge of something pours down my legs. My belly tightens, turning rock hard, and I grab onto it with both hands.

Sebastian instantly comes alert. "What's wrong, honey? Are you hurting again?" His hands skims over the tensed muscles in my back, pushing in with a light pressure that should have been relaxing, but it sent lightning bolts shredding through the base of my spine.

"I think my water just broke!" I led out a muffled whimper as the pressure tightened even further, the babies kicking out like they intended to break my skin. They were coming!

4

"Easy, now. Don't push too hard!" The never-ending pulse of the contractions squeezed down on my belly, pushing the first baby down my birth canal way too fast. Sebastian's fingers slips inside my lips, his eyes narrowing in deep thought as I can feel three of them slide right up to the hilt. My lips thin in a tight smile, sweat starting to trickle down my neck again as each passing heartbeat pulled me open wider. Each second closer to the babies sliding out of me. "You're pretty wide. Maybe eight or nine centimeters?" He finally says, my core clenching down on the invasion of his fingers.

My lips pulled back in a grimace, the large head of the first baby grating against my bones as it slid down. The insistent need to push never ceased as the contractions grew stronger, pressing down on my huge swollen belly until it felt like I would rip apart. I needed to breath, but the other two babies still waiting higher in my belly squirmed so hard that it stole my breath away. I sobbed, tears streaming down my face like a warm river. I can't do this.

"Easy, honey. You've almost got the first one out." Sebastian shifts, one strong arm pulling me into the support of his chest while the other curves around my belly. His fingers still trail over my swollen slit, confirming what his eyes can't see for me, and it starts to feel different from the pressure down there. Like I'm bulging. Another contraction leaves me screaming in pain and pushing as hard as I could. My toes curl under, my spine arching high, and my twitching overfull belly pushes up into the air from the power of an intense throb down below. "I can feel the head!

Keep going!" He chatters in my ear, ghosting his lips against my forehead, and my lips feel like they're on fire.

I can feel my lips bulging out into the telltale teardrop shape in his hand, the contractions forcing everything open faster than it normally should. It's too much. Everything burns. It was too big, I couldn't stretch anymore. Sebastian murmurs something, but it's drowned out with my shriek as the red hot cramp reaches another peak. It's the worst one yet. The pain so blinding that blackness dances around the edge of my vision. His fingers flutter, tugging something out of me, and I barely hear him whisper something about a head.

Was it out?

"Good job! Keep going!" I force myself to listen to him despite how my body heaves. I push down again, my hands crushing the fabric of the sofa, and something slips free in a squirt of moisture. The sudden absence of weight hurts almost as much as the ache of the babies high in my belly still coming.

"It's a boy!" He nearly shouts, quickly lifting the fluid soaked baby up to my chest. I blink blearily, the unfamiliar wriggling weight so foreign but yet I could see both myself and Sebastian in his tiny features. I wanted to hold him, but another cramp lances through my belly, and I can feel his sibling sliding into place. Ready to be born just as quickly as he was.

"Just hold him for me. The second one's coming!" I growled.

5

"Hold on! Here we go." Sebastian runs into the bathroom and grabs a towel, cursing under his breath as he tries to wrap the baby up, but the wriggling limbs keep getting caught in the folds of the towel. It brings a brief smile to my face. I say brief because the next flutter of movement inside was drowned out by the clamping pain of the contractions. The desperate urge to push, to force this life out of me, becomes too strong.

Then came the stretching, the tight feeling of something pulling me open again. Coming even faster than the first, the second scraped down my canal so fast that I could barely suck in a breath. Each heartbeat had it moving closer to crowning.

"Sebastian, hurry!" A fleshy thump made me raise my head, and I glanced over towards the door to see him scrambling back to his feet.

"Got it, our boy is settled for now. But he needs his mama soon." Sliding to a stop at my parted thighs, Sebastian knelt down and started to rub the rock hard dome of my still swollen belly. "You're doing so good. How many more do you think are in there?"

"At l-least two!" I screamed, throwing my head back against the support of the sofa with the power of the push. My belly arched up into his hands from sheer force, the ache in my hips slipping lower with every breath. Soon the fire started to burn my lips, consuming the stretched tissues with a familiar pain.

"Damn! And here comes number two. Give me your hand." Loosening my grip on the sofa, I reach out and trail my fingers over his wrist. His long fingers guided my own through the swollen slickness of my bulging lips, and something moist lingered just behind my entrance. My baby's head. A single tear traced down my cheek. My reason for all this pain. It was almost out, another few pushes and I could hold it. "You feel it? The baby's head?" I glanced up and saw Sebastian's eyes shining with pride, so much pride and affection that I felt like I would drown in a sea of his love.

"Yeah. Baby's coming." I wish I could say that I loved it already, that I loved him, but the quickly intensifying pain ripped away any speech I had. The pushing, shoving, tight feeling ripping through me like a wave, and I screamed so loud that my throat felt raw. Then one by one, I could feel the baby slipping out. The head, the shoulders, Sebastian's gentle fingers tracing around the body and guiding it out into his waiting hands. I was tired. So, so tired and raw, but then the weight slipped free.

I sagged back against the sofa in relief, the momentary lull of the contractions leaving the muscles in my swollen belly twitching from overuse. My last little one still squirmed deep inside me, thrashing against my belly as it rolled and kicked. A wave of exhaustion crashing down on my body, ripping apart the last shreds of strength I had. The tug of the contractions did little to push it away, the constant pain more of a lullaby than anything.

"Honey?" Warm hands weave around my back, the sofa dipping as he somehow pulls my sweaty, filthy body against his chest. "Hey, now! You gotta stay awake. There's one more still to come." His lips ghost against my cheek, demanding my attention no matter how tired I am. I can hear the babies faintly crying in the distance, their sibling still squirming inside my belly as it tried to push its way out.

"Can't." The word sluggishly falls from my lips. I'm just so tired. I need to sleep now. Then the baby can come out. Later.

"I'm sorry, sweetheart. But you've got to wake up." The vague pressure of his hand slid from my back, rounding up and over the tense muscles in my shoulders, before cupping the weight of my breasts. A small squeak slips out when his fingers flick the sensitive surface of my nipples, and then my eyes fly wide open as they pinch together.

Instead of the pleasure that I usually found in Sebastian's hands, a flood of a feeling so intense that my core instantly clenched down on the baby, prolonging my current contraction. I whine, thrashing my head back and forth against his chest while my spine arches, pushing my chest further into his delightful torture. "I heard that nipple stimulation helps when a woman is in labor. Guess it works pretty good, huh?" His raspy chuckle vibrated against my ear, streams of warm milk pouring over his knuckles while he kneaded my breasts.

"Pretty knowledgeable about- THIS! Are you?" Torn between screaming and crying, the exhausted muscles in my core relentlessly shove the baby down my canal. The tell-tale burning started again, and I sighed in somewhat relief that the baby was beginning to crown.

"Just a little thing I was curious about for the future. I sure wasn't expecting to come home and find you pregnant. Guess I did a pretty good job last time to knock you up with three babies." A moan slips out, thick and hot just like the curl of arousal pooling low in my belly. Reaching back behind me, my fingernails trail along the soft skin of his inner thigh. The shiver that ripples through his body makes me wish I could flip him over right now and ride him until he's screaming. The press of his soft cock vaguely twitching against my aching lower back only enhancing that. "Not right now. This isn't about me." His voice deepens with a thick coat of lust, that special bedroom voice that always gets me dripping wet no matter what. "This is about you.

I need you to cum now, and bring our baby into this world. Now cum!"

It still works. A twin shot of pleasure and pain ripping my body open and tearing my head right off my body. My muscles contract, something popping free down below, and I'm gasping for air as the twitching aftershocks rotate and twist the baby right out of me. My heart's pounding, racing through my ears like thunder, and drowns out whatever Sebastian was saying to me. The dark blackness creeps in behind my eyes, blotting out everything, and now I feel like I can just sleep.

Sometime later, I woke up to the gentle nuzzle of a soft cheek against my breasts. Full of milk again, the steady pull of a tiny tongue lapping at each nipple made my eyes flutter open. A little boy and a girl were each attached to either side of my chest, sucking hungrily while their tiny chubby forms kicked and squirmed in delight. A smile folded up each side of my lips, my arms curling around the precious little bundles of joy that had taken me by surprise. But where was the other one, and Sebastian too?

And how did I get into our bedroom?

"Hey, sounds like someone is awake." Strolling into the bedroom with our third little one cradled against his chest, the bed dipped as Sebastian crawled up beside me. "I was starting to wonder when you would wake up."

"Sorry, popping out three little ones is pretty exhausting." I glanced down at the sweet little faces all around me, my heart swelling up so full that I thought I would bust. "Thanks for the cleanup job, by the way."

"Honey, when have I not cleaned you up after sex? This wasn't any different, just that it had a surprise ending."

Speaking of surprise endings. That made me think about something he said before. "Sebastian, how did you know about a rapid pregnancy before?"

He tipped his head to the side, a stray strand of hair shifting forward to dangle in front of his eyes as he thought back. "Oh, that! I heard it on the radio as my driver was coming in. Something about a local pizza joint adding a special ingredient that made any person already pregnant go through a rapid pregnancy. Some kind of mix up in supplies or something." He shrugged his broad shoulders. "I don't really know the whole story."

Huh, that does explain a lot. Although... I wonder if we might could get a second special pizza to go? They always freeze pretty well, at least until I was recovered from this round anyway.

Don't miss out!

Visit the website below and you can sign up to receive emails whenever Talia Swarky publishes a new book. There's no charge and no obligation.

https://books2read.com/r/B-A-TGFK-VYGQB

BOOKS 2 READ

Connecting independent readers to independent writers.

About the Author

A lover of the sensual side of things with a twist of fantasy, she is a writer of dreams and fantasies.

You can connect with her on Tumblr at https://midnightfantasiesanddaydreams.tumblr.com/

Read more at https://books2read.com/ap/nBkZpK/Talia-Swarky.